Rylan and Bec

written by

G. Neubauer Kniefel

Cast of Characters

RYLAN - a 17 year old with social introversion.
BEC - a 16 year old with alcoholism.
BOBBY - a black 17 year old with anger issues.
KELLY - a 17 year old objectophiliac, a mother like figure.
CHELSEA - a 16 year old, not dissimilar from Regina George.
LEXI - a 20 something staff member at the treatment center. Preferably female, but can be played by a male.
JASON - a mid 20s to early 30s manager of the treatment center.

This play is dedicated to the memory of Robert Eugene Kniefel, a loving grandfather, a creative supporter, and an absolute titan.

SCENE 1: TREATMENT CENTER COMMON AREA

White walls. Two couches. A white board. A table. The white boards reads "May 6th" and the daily schedule. Kelly sits at the table shuffling cards. Bec sits across from her.

KELLY

You're terrified, aren't you?

BEC

I don't know what you're talking about.

KELLY

It's okay. This is a safe space. You don't have to pretend here.

BEC

I'm not pretending.

KELLY

Okay. I believe you.

BEC

I'm just... tired.

KELLY

I understand. I remember my first day here. I was so scared. I thought everyone was going to make fun of me.

BEC

Why would they make fun of you?

KELLY

Because the reason why I'm here is a little different than most.

BEC

Why are you here?

KELLY

I'll tell you my story if you tell me yours.

BEC

I'm not very comfortable with that.

KELLY

What if I promised I wouldn't judge you?

BEC

I don't know. I don't even know your name.

KELLY

My name is Kelly.

Kelly sticks out her hand.

BEC

Bec.

They shake hands.

KELLY
The big game on unit is Rummy. Do you know how to play?

BEC
Uh. Yeah, my family taught me when I was a kid.

Kelly deals 7 cards to the both of them.

BEC
How long have you been here?

KELLY
4 months. They keep pushing my discharge back.

BEC
Why?

KELLY
I'm not entirely sure. Nobody tells me anything.

BEC
That must be annoying.

KELLY
Oh yeah. I love everyone knowing everything about my discharge before I do.

BEC
What do you have to do to leave this place anyway?

KELLY
Depends on the person. I might be in limbo, but my plan will differ from yours. Generally, good behavior and working on certain goals will fulfill the requirements.

Bobby walks in with a broom.

BOBBY
Holy shit, the new girl is here.

KELLY
Bobby, this is Bec. Please try to avoid hitting on her.

BOBBY
You know I don't make promises I can't keep.

BEC
I have a boyfriend, but only if you're trying to make a move.

BOBBY
Nah, fam. Ain't like that. Let's just keep it cool between us, yeah?

Bobby holds out a fist. Bobby and Bec fist bump. Bobby turns to start sweeping.

BOBBY
Kell Bells, this ain't the one you put in your pussy, right, hon?

BEC
Wait, you use that broom as a dildo?

KELLY
(sighing)
No, Bobby. Shannon is a mop. And we have signs set up for her, unless Lexi took them down.

BEC
You named your mop Shannon?

KELLY
Yes.

BEC
Why?

KELLY
That's my thing. Objectophilia.

BEC
Objecto-whatia?

BOBBY
Kelly is in love with a mop named Shannon.

BEC
That's a thing?

KELLY
Yes, dear.

BEC
Holy shit.

BOBBY
I think it's fucking hilarious.

BEC
I mean, I wouldn't say that.

KELLY
Thank you, Bec. Bobby has been giving me a hard time about it for months.

BOBBY
Come on, I only tease ya because I love ya.

Bobby finishes sweeping and puts the broom down.

BEC
Rummy.

Bec picks up a pile of cards from the center of the table and puts it on her side.

BOBBY
So, Bec, what cocktail of mental instability has you joining us for an extended stay at the Loony Bin?

BEC
Can we maybe not get into it?

BOBBY
Fair enough.

BEC
I'm sorry, guys. It has nothing to do with you. I just... ugh.

KELLY
Don't apologize. We get it.

BOBBY
We'll just have to interrogate the other new inmate joining us.

BEC
They're already admitting another person?

BOBBY
We're always full. Five beds for five kids. As long as I've been here, each bed has been taken.

BEC
Wait then who's the fifth person?

KELLY
Her name is Chelsea. She likes to spend her free time in her room, alone.

BEC
Why?

BOBBY
Deems us unworthy. Her loss because this unit is a glorious and fucking hysterical shit show.

Lexi enters with Rylan.

LEXI
And this is our day room. This is where most of our day takes place. You'll be receiving levels, doing chores, eating meals, and spending free time while on unit here. Do you have any questions?

Rylan shakes his head no.

LEXI
Perfect. Everyone, this is Rylan, our newest resident. Please be aware that he is unable to speak, so let's try our best to navigate that. Hopefully, we can change that soon.

Rylan looks at her angrily.

LEXI

Anyway, let's put the cards up and get ready for lunch. Jason's been cooking all morning. I'm going to go grab Chelsea.

Lexi exits. Rylan sits down cautiously on the couch.

KELLY

Rylan?

Rylan looks at her scared.

KELLY

You want to come sit with us?

Rylan shakes his head no.

BOBBY

Aw, come on, you cock tease. We don't bite hard.

Rylan looks scared.

BEC

Leave him be. He's probably scared shitless right now.

Rylan relaxes a little. Kelly starts cleaning up her cards. Chelsea enters, in a bold and outlandish way.

CHELSEA

So I hear there are new inmates joining the ranks today.

KELLY

Chelsea, this is Rylan and Bec.

CHELSEA

Ah, yes. Welcome to Purgatory.

KELLY

Oh, don't tell them that.

CHELSEA

What? I only speak the truth.

KELLY

That doesn't mean come in and demoralize them! Your experience will probably be different from theirs.

CHELSEA

Only warning of the horrors to come. Lights out at 9, prison food, forced family therapy!

BEC

Seems a bit dramatic don't you think?

Chelsea snaps her head around to her.

CHELSEA
You should learn to watch your tongue.

BEC
You should suck my dick.

CHELSEA
(a bit more malicious)
I figured someone in your position would appreciate an inside perspective.

BEC
I'd like to form my own opinion, if that's cool.

For a moment, they look like they're going to fight. Then out of nowhere, Chelsea starts laughing.

CHELSEA
I like YOU. You got a toothier bite than most of the other societal rejects in here.

KELLY
Hey! I am not a reject.

CHELSEA
(to Kelly, slightly condescendingly)
Cute! Love ya, Kel.

Jason enters with a big pot of food.

JASON
Guys, didn't Lexi ask you guys to clean up for lunch?

KELLY
Yep. Sorry, Jason.

JASON
Well, let's get to it. Whose chore is it to set the table?

CHELSEA
Mine.

JASON
Let's hop on it, yeah?

CHELSEA
I'll get to it.

Jason sees Bec.

JASON
You must be Rebecca.

BEC
I prefer Bec.

JASON
My apologies. I'm Jason. I'm the manager of this unit and one of the live-in staff.

BEC
Nice to meet you.

CHELSEA
Don't get caught doing anything around him, fresh meat. He's a real pain in the ass when it comes to following the rules.

JASON
Chelsea. Come on, let's put a little pep in our step, yeah?

CHELSEA
Quit your babbling, plebeian.

JASON
Do you want to be level one again tomorrow?

Chelsea makes a motion as though a butterfly was flying away from her.

CHELSEA
Oh no, there goes my final fuck.

JASON
Level one it is.

CHELSEA
Fantastic!

Chelsea walks out.

JASON
Bobby, you're level one, right? Do you think you could set the table as an extra chore?

BOBBY
I fucking love how you assume that shit, man. I could be level four for all you know.

JASON
That language is telling me otherwise.

BOBBY
Fine. I'll set your goddamn table.

Bobby and Jason walk into the kitchen.

BEC
What was he talking about with levels?

KELLY
Levels determine privileges. Level one and two mean extra chores. Level three and four mean outings and being priv'd.

BEC
Oh. What does being priv'd mean?

KELLY
It means you get access to the priv room where there are movies and video games. Plus you need to be priv'd to go out on pass. Bobby has the wonderful habit of being level one everyday, so he hasn't left the center in a long while.

BEC
Is it because he cusses so much?

KELLY
Among other things. He's the reason we have to replace the bookshelf every week and a half.

Bobby reenters with a stack of paper plates.

BOBBY
Jesus, Kelly, they've been here 10 minutes and you're already telling them my life story.

BEC
Relax, big guy. She didn't say anything bad.

BOBBY
Sure. And my black ass bout to be fuckin' Kate Upton.

BEC
I'm not sure asses can fuck anything.

BOBBY
Why are all your responses so quippy? Shit's annoying.

KELLY
Chill out, Bobby.

BOBBY
Telling me to chill pisses me off more. It's the same shit as telling your girl to chill when she catches you balls deep in her dog.

Everyone looks at him with a "what the fuck?" face.

BOBBY
Not that I would know about that or anything ...

Rylan gets up and sits over by Bec. He tries to avert eye contact. Bec turns to him slightly.

BEC
Your first day too, huh?

Rylan looks up, nods solemnly.

BEC
Well, good luck. We're gonna need it.

Rylan relaxes a little.

SCENE 2: RYLAN'S BEDROOM

There are two beds in the room. Rylan sits at the desk in the room, reading a book. Bobby enters, wearing shorts and a tank top.

BOBBY
Ah. Right. Forgot that you now sleep 10 feet away from where I jerk off.

Rylan looks grossed out.

BOBBY
Relax. I don't moan that loud.

Bobby walks over and thumps Rylan on the back. This triggers Rylan's fight or flight response. His body tenses up and starts blinking rapidly.

BOBBY
Whoa, dude. You good?

Rylan is wide eyed, but nods.

BOBBY
My bad. I was just tryna pat you on the back.

Rylan nods.

BOBBY
Right, you don't talk, do you?

Rylan just looks at him.

BOBBY
Fuck, alright.

Bobby sits on his bed. Rylan starts to change into pajamas. We see scars on his back.

BOBBY
Whoa, where the fuck did you get those?

Rylan averts eye contact and quickly starts to redress.

BOBBY
Never mind. That's none of my business.

They both get into their respective beds and get under the covers.

BOBBY
Could you turn the lights out?

Rylan nods and does so. They both start to fall asleep.

BLACK OUT

SCENE 3: RYLAN'S BEDROOM

Middle of the night immediately following the previous scene. Bobby and Rylan are asleep. Suddenly, Rylan wakes up, screaming. Bobby wakes up, startled. He gets up and opens the door.

BOBBY
(yelling out)
Can we get someone in here please?

Jason enters.

JASON
(soothingly)
Hey, hey. Rylan, you're okay. You're safe.

Rylan is crying but stops screaming.

BOBBY
Dude, what happened?

JASON
Bobby, do you think you could do me a favor and go out into the common area? I want to give Rylan some space.

BOBBY
Nah, fuck that, he's my roommate. I want to know what's going on with him.

JASON
Bobby. Please.

Bobby grumbles, but exits.

JASON
Glad to know your vocal cords work.

Rylan nods.

JASON
I'm not going to try to get you to talk, but I need you to answer a few yes or no questions for me. Can you do that?

Rylan nods.

JASON
Nightmare?

Rylan nods.

JASON

Are these types of things consistent?

Rylan nods.

JASON

I'll make note of that.

Rylan shakes his head no.

JASON

I have to. It's my job.

Rylan blinks.

JASON

I'm sorry. I know you don't like that, but we need to be aware of it so we can better prepare ourselves for the next time this happens.

Rylan slowly nods.

JASON

Was it a bad memory? Sometimes, when we suffer from abuse, we have nightmares about it.

Rylan starts to shut down.

JASON

Hey, it's okay. We don't have to talk about it.

Rylan closes his eyes and breathes deeply.

JASON

I know what you're feeling.

Rylan looks up at him.

JASON

I've seen kids come through here for the better part of two years. I've seen what the transition does to people.

Rylan nods.

JASON

It sucks being away from everything you know. Family, friends, safety and comfort of your own life.

Rylan nods.

JASON

I know it's tough, but we're here to help you. Even if you don't believe it, the staff here want what's best for the residents.

Rylan nods.

JASON

Are you going to be okay?

Rylan nods.

JASON
Okay. Try to get some rest, yeah?

Rylan nods.

JASON
I'll see you in the morning.

Jason walks off. Rylan starts to relax. Bobby comes back in.

BOBBY
Shit, dude, you good?

Rylan nods.

BOBBY
Fuck, you scared the shit outta me, man. I was having a good dream too. I was playin' with Kate Upton's .... anyway, I was not ready for that.

Rylan shrugs.

BOBBY
Yeah, alright. Get some sleep, bitch ass. Tomorrow the real fun begins.

Bobby gets into bed.

BLACK OUT

SCENE 4: TREATMENT CENTER COMMON AREA

The board reads "May 24th". Rylan and Bec are sitting on the couch. Lexi, Bobby, Kelly, and Chelsea are putting on jackets and tying shoes.

BEC
Lexi, I still don't understand why Rylan and I can't go on the outing tonight.

LEXI
Unfortunately, you didn't put in your request for you to be taken off community restriction until after the team meeting, so now you and Rylan are both restricted to the community.

KELLY
It's okay, Bec. You'll be able to go on the next one.

BOBBY
No shit, but they ain't going to fuckin' Avengers like we are!

LEXI
Bobby, if I hear one more curse word, you will be level one tomorrow, I swear.

Bobby shuts his mouth.

CHELSEA
Can we get out of here? I'm losing sympathy for them by the second.

KELLY
Be nice, Chelsea. It wasn't too long ago that you were in their shoes.

CHELSEA
Yeah, but at least I actually knew how to use my mouth and could talk to everyone.

Chelsea glares at Rylan.

LEXI
Chelsea, that's enough. Rylan, Bec, Jason is in the office if you need him.

BEC
Thank you, Lexi.

Lexi, Bobby, Kelly, and Chelsea exit.

BEC
(holding up a pack of cards)
Rummy?

Rylan nods. They move to the table.

BEC
Goddamn Avengers. It isn't even all that great of a movie anyway.

Rylan shrugs. Bec shuffles the cards and deals them out.

BEC
Were you a big movie fan growing up?

Rylan nods, though it's closer to an "eh" reaction.

BEC
Not your jam?

Rylan shakes his head no.

BEC
Yeah, I understand. Movies aren't for everyone, but I've always loved them. I used to want to be in them.

Rylan looks at her curiously.

BEC
Yeah, when I was 13, I'd take my phone and record goofy little videos. It was a lot of fun. I remember this one time, I was acting in some shitty Star Wars rip off and my friend Davie was holding the phone. I was messing around with this stick pretending that it was a lightsaber. He didn't back up when I was swinging it around and I accidentally hit him in the eye. I felt really bad about it.

Rylan nods, processing the information.

BEC
Sorry. I just realized how awful that sounds.

Rylan shakes his head, trying to dispel her worries.

BEC
What do you want to be when you grow up?

Rylan thinks for a moment, then simply smiles.

BEC
A comedian?

Rylan shakes his head no. He points to himself then smiles again.

BEC
Oh, you want to be happy.

Rylan nods.

BEC
Cute.

Rylan slaps the table, calling rummy.

BEC
Fuck.

Rylan scoops up the cards and they keep playing.

BEC
Made any break throughs in therapy, yet?

Rylan shakes his head no.

BEC
Have you even spoken with your therapist?

Rylan shakes his head no.

BEC
I'm sorry. I don't mean to pry.

Rylan shrugs.

BEC
Are you doing okay?

Rylan simply looks at her.

BEC
Sorry.

Rylan motions towards her, asking "how are you doing?"

BEC

How am I doing?

Rylan nods.

BEC

Do you actually care?

Rylan nods, confused expression on his face.

BEC

I know it's weird, I've just been burned out by some people.

Rylan understands.

BEC

To answer your question, I'm... I don't know. Sad. Pissed. Tired.

Rylan nods.

BEC

I miss my friends. But I could never tell them I was in here. What would they think of me? They'd think I'm fucking nuts. They would leave me in the dust.

Rylan nods.

BEC

It sucks. I feel like there's no one in my life who I can just talk to. My friends would judge me. My parents are fucking nonexistent. I'd rather be stuck in a German sex dungeon and have forgotten the safe word than talk to any of the staff here.

Rylan nods.

BEC

I hate everything. I'm missing the Snowball dance this weekend. I was actually kind of excited. Maybe because it was my last Snowball, but it just meant something else this time, ya know?

Rylan nods.

BEC

Instead, I have to be stuck here in a stupid mental health unit because someone "decided" that's what's best for me. No one asked my opinion. Nobody cared that I thought I was doing fine. They just shipped me off to the rehab center on 4th avenue. Fuck treatment.

Rylan nods, then motions "One moment," and starts to walk off stage.

BEC

Where are you going?

Rylan points a finger off stage, then walks out. He returns with a CD player and a speaker.

BEC
Oh, right. I forgot those were a thing. We can have these here?

Rylan nods. He puts the speaker down, then plugs in the CD player. He presses play and "A Beautiful Mess" by Jason Mraz starts playing. Rylan takes Bec's hand.

BEC
What are you doing?

Rylan motions for her to stand. She does, and they start dancing.

BEC
Oh. O-okay.

Rylan leads her in a choreographed dance, because of course the quiet dude knows how to dance. Bec is astonished with Rylan's ability. Eventually they slow down and slow dance together for a minute. Bec lays her head on his shoulders.

BEC
Thank you.

Rylan nods. Jason enters.

JASON
Guys, boundaries. Come on.

They break apart.

BEC
Sorry, Jason. He was just helping me out with something.

JASON
Just... don't do it again.

BEC
Promise.

JASON
Rylan?

Rylan nods.

JASON
Okay. Next time, you both will be level one, okay?

BEC
Okay.

Jason exits.

BLACK OUT

SCENE 5: TREATMENT CENTER COMMON AREA

The board reads "May 30th". All the residents sit on the couches. Rylan stands in front of Lexi, who is reading from a binder.

LEXI

Level 3, and your request to be taken off of community restriction has been approved. You are now eligible for outings and pass, but please keep boundaries with peers a priority.

Rylan nods and takes a seat next to Bobby. Lexi closes her binder.

LEXI

Well, that's it for levels. Please don't go too far. Jason is leading group in a few minutes.

CHELSEA

And what stupid topic have we decided on today?

LEXI

Resilience within a family setting.

Everyone except Rylan and Lexi collectively groans.

LEXI

Oh hush. It's not that bad.

BOBBY

Yeah, because asking a group of mentally ill teenagers about their abusive and toxic parents is a fucking great idea.

LEXI

Bobby, please keep the negative comments to yourself. And watch your language. You'll be level one again tomorrow if you don't.

Lexi takes the binder and leaves. Bobby flips her off when she's off stage.

BOBBY

Fuckin' bitch. I hate that she has to make some sort of comment to make me feel shitty. It's almost like she's threatening me.

CHELSEA

That's the thing, Bobert. She IS threatening you.

BOBBY

Fuckin' cunt.

Various forms of "fuck off", "Hey!", and "Whoa, whoa, whoa" come from the women in the room. Rylan merely flinches.

BEC

Kid, I don't give a fuck who you are or how much you think you're hot shit. Don't ever call someone a cunt.

BOBBY
Yeah, yeah, I'm sorry.

CHELSEA
If you're wondering, saying things like that is the reason you've never dicked anyone down.

BOBBY
I've fucked plenty of people.

BEC
You know who else says that?

CHELSEA
Virgins.

BOBBY
I ain't no fuckin' virgin. I've been fucking bitches since I was in middle school.

CHELSEA
If they're in middle school, they're not bitches. They're children.

BEC
Bobby, you've been fucking children? Is that why you're in here?

BOBBY
Fuck off, both of y'all.

KELLY
Guys, come on. Leave him alone.

CHELSEA
Or what?

KELLY
Or I'll tell Jason.

CHELSEA
Like I care. Why don't you let the grownups talk for a minute?

BOBBY
Fuck off already!

BEC
I'm sorry, I don't think I can listen to a pedophile.

CHELSEA
What would society think of a 16-year-old pedophile? That explains the court documents!

BOBBY
(shouting)
I SAID FUCK OFF.

The room goes quiet for a moment. Jason comes in.

JASON
What's going on in here? Bobby, why were you shouting?

BOBBY
(begrudgingly)
Nothing. I just got a little excited.

JASON
Oh. Okay, well, please try and watch the language.

BOBBY
Yeah, yeah.

JASON
Are we ready for group?

KELLY
Ready as we'll ever be, Jason.

JASON
Fantastic.

Jason writes "Family" on the board. Lexi reenters with a clipboard.

BOBBY
The fuck is she doing here?

LEXI
Watch the language. I'm a staff member. I go where I am needed.

JASON
My understanding is there was some push back when today's topic was revealed, so I figured Lexi would sit in and make notes of any attempted disruptions. Today's group will be reflected in tomorrow's points, so if we could remain on topic, that would be appreciated.

Lexi smirks pointedly at Bobby. He mutters something under his breath.

LEXI
What was that?

BOBBY
Nothing.

JASON
So. A lot of times, when residents are admitted here, one of the biggest issues they deal with has to do with their home life. There are numerous kinds of family, whether those who are related to you by blood or the family you choose in a group of friends. I thought today we would talk about what our own home lives look like and how we personally deal with frustrations within them.

BEC
Jason, I really don't know how comfortable I am talking about my family.

LEXI

You will discuss it or you won't get points for the group.

JASON

I think what Lexi means to say is we will talk about however much is comfortable to you. You know your limits.

BEC

Well... I mean I guess.

KELLY

I can go first if you guys would like.

JASON

Sure! Awesome. Show us how it's done

KELLY

Well, I live with my mom and dad. They're still together after 26 years and 2 kids.

JASON

Good for them. Do you have a sibling too?

KELLY

Yeah, my little brother, Jamie. He's 11.

JASON

Okay, what are some of the challenges you face with your family? Do you argue with your brother a lot?

KELLY

No, Jamie and I get along pretty well. My parents are a different story.

CHELSEA

Pray tell, young mop fucker.

LEXI

(menacingly)

Chelsea.

Chelsea rolls her eyes.

KELLY

My parents have kinda treated me different since I came out to them.

JASON

What do you mean?

KELLY

Well... they sent me here.

BEC

Excuse me?

KELLY

Yeah. I never had an easy time with them beforehand. I was socially awkward, I spent a lot of time alone with my books rather than going out and spending time with friends. I tried to be better about that, but making friends was hard for me. They pushed and pushed for me to get out there, but it just made me anxious. When I came out to them, they thought that there was something wrong with me so they sent me here.

BEC

Oh, Kelly.

KELLY

No, no, it's fine. There probably is good reason for being in here.

BEC

Just because your sexuality is different?

KELLY

Well... yeah, loving inanimate objects is wrong.

BEC

Says who?

Silence.

JASON

Well, who would like to go next?

Nobody raises their hand.

LEXI

Chelsea seems like she's ready.

Chelsea stares daggers at Lexi.

CHELSEA

No, I'd like to provide an opportunity for our newer residents to share intimate information.

LEXI

Points are dropping.

CHELSEA

(groaning)

Fine. Daddy's a heart surgeon and Mommy's the trophy wife. We live in the nice part of town with our pup, Scooter.

JASON

And what are some problems that tend to arise within your household?

CHELSEA

Scooter poops on the rug sometimes.

Bec slightly chuckles.

CHELSEA

(to Bec)

Was that funny?

BEC
No. But if that's the worst problem to come through your house, I would consider yourself very luck.

CHELSEA
My issues do not lie within the confines of my home. I have a fantastic relationship with my parents.

JASON
Then why hide that? You seemed hesitant to open up.

CHELSEA
Yes, because I don't like juvenile delinquents to know my personal information.

BOBBY
Guess what, babe? You're one of us too.

LEXI
Bobby, you seem to have something to say. Why don't you share with the group about your family?

BOBBY
Nah.

LEXI
Oh, and why is that?

BOBBY
It doesn't matter.

LEXI
You and I both know it does.

JASON
Lexi...

LEXI
Shhh. Let me handle this.
(turns to Bobby)
Why don't you want to talk about them? And don't play with me.

BOBBY
I ain't playin'. Shit doesn't matter.

LEXI
You tell lies almost as much as you curse.

BEC
Lexi, stop. That's not fair.

LEXI
Did I say it was your turn, Bec?

Bec falls silent. Bobby grows flustered.

LEXI
What are you hiding, Bobby? Is Momma mean to you?

BOBBY
I don't need to answer that.

LEXI
Why not? Because you're afraid it's true?

JASON
Lexi…

LEXI
I can handle this.

Bobby doesn't respond.

LEXI
What's wrong? Don't want to talk about Daddy beating you?

BOBBY
Fuck you, you stupid bitch. How dare you bring that shit up! How dare you try and pull information out of me and bring up shit in my past, especially in front of my peers. You have no fucking right. Who are you to come in and tell me my truth? You are nothing but a sadistic, spineless vermin.

LEXI
Don't you dare talk to me like that.

BOBBY
I'll say whatever I want. You're fucking insane.

LEXI
That's enough, Bobby. Please go to your room and practice your coping skills.

BOBBY
You don't get to tell me when enough is enough. You are done telling me what to do.

Bobby starts throwing books at Lexi. Jason puts Bobby into a hold.

LEXI
I'm getting the sedative.

BOBBY
(screaming)
Fuck your booty juice you fucking cunt.

JASON
(struggling to hold Bobby)
Guys, can we move to the priv room please?

Rylan, Bec, Chelsea, and Kelly all exit.

BOBBY
(screaming)
Fuck you, you cuck. You don't have the balls to stand up to Lexi because you're afraid of losing your job.

JASON
Bobby, don't make this harder than it already is.

Bobby spits in Jason's face.

BOBBY
Fuck you.

Lexi walks back in with a syringe.

LEXI
Well, let's get this over with.

Jason holds Bobby down as Lexi pulls his pants down.

BOBBY
GET OFF ME. GET THE FUCK OFF. NO. NO. NO!

Lexi sticks the syringe in Bobby's ass.

BOBBY
Fuck you, Lexi. Fuck you.

LEXI
I'm sorry, Bobby.

JASON
It's gonna be alright.

BOBBY
(to Jason, while relaxing)
You're a pussy.

JASON
Okay.

Bobby stops fighting and relaxes.

BLACK OUT

SCENE 6: RYLAN'S BEDROOM

Bobby is tampering with the security system on the window. Rylan enters. He looks at Bobby incredulously.

BOBBY
What?

Rylan nods at the security system Bobby is fiddling with.

BOBBY

Nah, man, I'm just tryna figure this out so I can go smoke a blunt. It ain't no thing.

Rylan looks disappointed.

BOBBY

Oh, come on, man. This ain't that big of a deal.

Rylan shakes his head.

BOBBY

Whatever.

Bobby continues to mess with it. There is a knock on the door. Bobby jumps, steps back from the window.

BOBBY

Yeah?

Bec enters.

BEC

(to Bobby)

Hey.

BOBBY

(Rolls his eyes)

The fuck do you want?

BEC

Can I come in?

BOBBY

No.

BEC

Please?

BOBBY

I said no. And that ain't cuz of me. Lexi and Jason would shit themselves if they found out you came in here.

BEC

Can we talk?

BOBBY

(sighing)

Kick it in the doorway.

Bec leans onto the doorway.

BEC

I'm sorry.

BOBBY

Fuck outta here.

BEC

I'm serious.

BOBBY

Bitch, no you aren't.

BEC

Don't call me a bitch.

BOBBY

Sorry. Would you prefer ma'am?

BEC

Ma'am makes me sound like I'm trying to see the manager. Too Karen for me.

BOBBY

Look, can you just get the fuck outta here?

Bec slumps down.

BEC

What are you doing?

BOBBY

Fucking your sister. What does it look like I'm doing?

BEC

It looks like you're trying to figure out how to break out.

BOBBY

Glad you aren't as stupid as you look.

BEC

Oh come on, that was cheap.

BOBBY

Kinda like making fun of someone for being a virgin and then callin' them a pedo right after?

Bec shifts uncomfortably.

BEC

Yeah... I'm sorry about that.

BOBBY

I don't need your half assed apologies.

BEC

No, I really am. Especially with what happened after. I wouldn't have said anything if -

BOBBY

(interrupting)

If you had known you were part of the reason I blew out?

BEC
(hesitantly)
Well... yeah.

BOBBY
Look, I have enough girls who treat me like shit on a regular basis, I don't have time for another one.

BEC
Oh, come on, Bobby. Please.

BOBBY
I'm for real. I ain't about you comin' in and treating me like shit just cause I'm different than you.

BEC
You're not that diff-

BOBBY
Oh get the fuck outta here. You know that's not true.

BEC
Just because we have different backgrounds doesn't mean -

BOBBY
Lemme ask you something. Were you stuck out in the shitty parts of town? Were you beaten and belittled by the very people who brought you onto this earth? Were you made fun of at school because your clothes were old and raggy because instead of taking you to Goodwill to get something that actually fits, your parents use the money to buy booze? Nah, I think the fuck not.

BEC
How about you actually ask me if those things happen instead of assuming that they haven't.

BOBBY
Well, did they?

BEC
Yes. You're not the only one who has been abused by their parents and you thinking so is ignorant.

They stare at each other.

BOBBY
(slowly)
Fair enough.

BEC
Genuinely, I am sorry. You didn't deserve any of that and I shouldn't be tied into Chelsea's bullying.

BOBBY
Yeah, aight.

BEC
Okay.

Bec notices Rylan for the first time.

BEC
Hey Rylan.

Rylan nods in greeting.

BOBBY
So you apologized, now get outta here.

BEC
Can you show me how to break out?

BOBBY
Now why the fuck would I do that?

BEC
Cause you feel bad for me?

BOBBY
Ah yes. I'm the one who should feel bad for you.

BEC
I just assume everyone does.

BOBBY
Fuck off.

BEC
Okay, how about because I need to go use some contraband?

BOBBY
Now, we're talking. What you got in your sock drawer?

BEC
A bottle of something.

BOBBY
Ahaha. Drinker, I see.

BEC
Well, yeah. Here and there at least.

BOBBY
Why not just swig it at night and hide it when they're doing night checks?

BEC
Dude, I am a loud ass drunk.

BOBBY
So you drink often?

BEC

Often enough to know how it affects me.

BOBBY
How often is that?

BEC
I don't want to answer that.

BOBBY
Why not?

BEC
Because it's personal.

BOBBY
I shared my shit. Lemme hear some of yours.

BEC
No.

BOBBY
Fuckin' hypocrite.

BEC
I am not!

BOBBY
(sarcastically)
Yeah, okay.

BEC
Who are you to say anything?

BOBBY
At least I own my shit. You'd rather act like there's nothing wrong with you.

BEC
There is nothing wrong with me!

BOBBY
Then how did you wind up in here?

BEC
Because... well... I kinda... totaled my car when I was drunk.

BOBBY
What?

BEC
Yeah. Turns out I wasn't good to drive. I'm pretty sure the guy I T-Boned would agree.

Silence.

BOBBY
Damn.

BEC

Yeah. The guy came out of it unscathed, but I was given the choice of jail time or treatment. I went with the one that would maybe give me a better future.

BOBBY

It's not an easy choice.

BEC

You were given the same?

BOBBY

Yeah, which is why Chels brought up court documents. I was caught setting my math teacher's lawn on fire. Mother fucker had cameras all over the front of the house.

BEC

Why your math teacher?

BOBBY

Cause he gave me an F on a test and Momma whipped my ass.

Bec nods in understanding.

BEC

Rylan?

Rylan looks up.

BEC

What about you?

BOBBY

Good luck gettin' it outta him. I don't know if you realized that he doesn't open his dick suckers up.

Rylan looks at him angrily, then takes his shirt off and shows his scars to Bec to spite him.

BEC

Holy shit.

BOBBY

I knew that was why.

Rylan jeers silently at him.

BEC

Was that... from your parents?

Rylan simply stares.

BOBBY

For what it's worth, I'm surprised you even got that much outta him.

Bobby finishes with the window alarm.

BOBBY
I got it.

BEC
Teach me.

Bobby shows her how.

BOBBY
Aight, but if you get caught, shit ain't coming back to me yeah?

BEC
Snitches get stitches.

BOBBY
Bet. Imma go smoke right quick. Tell Lexi I'm in the shitter.

Bobby hops out the window. Rylan motions outside.

BEC
Now?

Rylan shakes his head no.

BEC
When?

Rylan mimes "later".

BEC
So after bed?

Rylan nods.

BEC
Okay, yeah. You'll have to get over the fact that I'll prolly get drunk.

Rylan rolls his eyes and nods.

SCENE 7: THE WOODS

Bec is sitting on the ground, drinking vodka out of bottle hidden in a boot. We hear rustling as Bec drunkenly tenses up. Rylan walks through the brush. He stops and they stare at each other.

BEC
Hello, quiet boy.

Bec giggles. Rylan stares at her.

BEC
Oh, don't worry, you fucking mute. We're golden.

Rylan sighs and takes a seat on the log. Bec offers him the boot.

BEC

Belvedere?

Rylan shakes his head "No". He takes a pack of cigarettes out of his pocket.

BEC

Fuckin' Christ, you smoke?

Rylan nods his head.

BEC

What in the fuck? Why? Those things taste like shit!

Rylan shrugs.

BEC

Can I have a drag?

Rylan hands her the cigarette. She puffs deeply.

BEC

I only smoke cigarettes when I'm drunk. Otherwise, I prefer my tobacco out of a hookah.

Rylan takes the cigarette back. Bec takes another slug of vodka.

BEC

God, I hate this shit. I ever tell you I hate vodka?

Rylan shakes his head no.

BEC

Yeah, fuck this. This shit is awful. But goddamn it do I love feeling nothing.

Rylan raises an eyebrow at her.

BEC

What? I have my vices. You have yours. You're one to fuckin' talk. Puffin' on cheap cancer sticks. Who are you to judge me? What kind are you even smoking anyway?

Rylan hands her the pack.

BEC

Viceroys? Who the fuck smokes Viceroys? Why can't you smoke American Spirits like a normal person? At least then you can destroy your lungs and look like a man of class.

Rylan shakes his head and scoffs.

BEC

Oh hush. I'm just messing with you. Smoke your hipster cigarettes, Mac DeMarco.

Bec chuckles at her own joke.

RYLAN
I think that's enough vodka, Bec.

Bec stares at him incredulously.

BEC
Holy shit. You're talking!

Rylan rolls his eyes and takes another drag.

BEC
You're talking! You have a voice! And it's deep!

RYLAN
Were you expecting a Mickey Mouse voice?

BEC
I don't know. I just couldn't tell if your balls had dropped yet.

RYLAN
The peach fuzz wasn't any indication?

BEC
Excuse me for not paying attention to your stubby facial hair. I was trying to figure out what was going on in that head of yours.

RYLAN
Trust me, you don't want those answers.

BEC
You're so fucking weird. Why can't you just be more normal?

RYLAN
You're drunk.

BEC
I'm drunk. Pshhhhhhh. I could land a plane like this.

RYLAN
As entertaining as that would be, I'm not sure you're as sober as you think you are.

Rylan takes the boot from her.

BEC
Hey, give that back!

Rylan slips the bottle out of the boot. It is 75% gone.

RYLAN
Jesus, Bec, was this a full bottle when you came out here?

BEC
I don't have to answer that.

RYLAN
Why are you drinking so much booze?

BEC
You keep your cool by shutting your mouth. I keep mine by drinking a lot.

RYLAN
Are you an alcoholic?

BEC
Fuck you.

RYLAN
No judgement. Just curious.

BEC
Seriously, fuck you.

RYLAN
Alright, whatever.

Rylan puffs the cigarette one last time, gets up, crushes it beneath his foot, then starts to walk away.

BEC
Wait.

Rylan stops and turns back around.

RYLAN
Yes?

BEC
Why now? What's the great reasoning behind why Rylan... what's your last name?

RYLAN
Hayes.

BEC
Why Rylan Hayes decided to open his yapper?

RYLAN
(small chuckle)
Wouldn't you like to know.

BEC
Please? I'm sorry.

RYLAN
Every instinct I'm having is screaming for me to tell you to fuck off.

BEC

You can trust me.

RYLAN

It's not you I'm worried about trusting.

BEC

What do you mean?

RYLAN

Actually, let me revise that. I do worry about trusting you. But honestly, I trust myself even less than I trust you.

BEC

Oh. That sounds unhealthy.

RYLAN

Why do you think I'm in treatment?

BEC

I'm sure you have reasons.

RYLAN

And you think that the moment I open my mouth, I'm just going to tell you my whole life story?

BEC

Please?

RYLAN

Not tonight, Bec. You're drunk and I'm exhausted.

BEC

Can we talk about this tomorrow?

RYLAN

I don't know. Let's just play it by ear.

BEC

Okay.

RYLAN

Can I ask you a favor?

BEC

Sure.

RYLAN

Don't sneak in anymore vodka. You're not as subtle as you think you are.

BEC

What's that supposed to mean?

Rylan just looks at her.

BEC

Fuck it. Fine.

RYLAN

Thank you.

BEC

But only if you tell me why you started talking now.

RYLAN

Of course there's a catch.

BEC

What can I say? I get what I want.

RYLAN

Yes. That's the issue.

BEC

Would you really want to disappoint drunk me?

RYLAN

Wasn't exactly on my to do list tonight, though times have changed.

BEC

You're cute when you're a smart ass.

RYLAN

And you're trouble when you're drunk.

BEC

I'll accept that. Now start talking.

RYLAN

(sighing)

It was ... Jason Mraz that got me to start talking.

BEC

Jason Mraz?

RYLAN

He wrote the song we danced to that second or third week here.

BEC

Oh, right. During the Avengers outing.

RYLAN

Right. Dancing with you was... different. Good, but different. I wasn't expecting that.

BEC

That was like a month ago though. Why are you talking now?

RYLAN

Because I want to talk to you.

BEC

To me?

RYLAN

Yes. I like you.

BEC

Like me? The fuck is wrong with you?

RYLAN

What do you mean?

BEC

I'm me. Why would anyone like that?

RYLAN

I would say the same about myself.

BEC

Yeah, but you get away with it because of your boyish charm.

RYLAN

Boyish charm isn't sex appeal.

BEC

To some people it is.

RYLAN

Agree to disagree.

BEC

It is to me.

RYLAN

So you like me then?

BEC

Maybe a little bit?

RYLAN

That sounded confident.

BEC

Dude, I'm drunk! What do you expect me to do?

RYLAN

Alright, fair enough.

BEC

Are you going to talk tomorrow, so I can remember?

RYLAN

Would that make you happy?

BEC

Yes. Very much.

RYLAN

Then, yes.

BEC

Yay.

RYLAN
Do you think it'd be a little too middle school to ask you to be my girlfriend?

BEC
Of course. But it's sweet. I'll think about it.

RYLAN
That being said, we might have to wait until discharge.

BEC
Why?

RYLAN
Do you think it's a good idea to start a relationship while in treatment?

BEC
I've heard worse ideas.

RYLAN
I don't know. Are you prepared to mess with your discharge if we get caught?

BEC
I like how you think I'm just going to say yes.

RYLAN
That would make things easier.

BEC
What makes you say that?

RYLAN
I'm surprised I've made it this far into the conversation without fucking up.

BEC
What do you mean "this far"?

RYLAN
I've never been able to tell a girl that I liked her.

BEC
Oh.

RYLAN
Generally, my feelings are inconvenient for the other person.

BEC
I get that.

RYLAN

I don't know, I just have a hard time discussing any of my feelings. Back when I was seeing a therapist outside of here, he always told me that "feelings are meant to be felt, but not acted upon."

BEC

That's wrong.

RYLAN

What do you mean?

BEC

Fuck that shit. Just feel things. It doesn't matter what the world thinks. Whatever you fucking want to feel just let yourself feel it. If you're sad, own that shit. If you feel like you're interested in someone or have feelings for them, then let yourself feel it all. Don't stop yourself just because you're too scared to take the leap.

Rylan opens his mouth to say something, then decides not to try and verbalize it. For the first time in his life, he feels seen. They sit there for a moment.

RYLAN

We should head back.

BEC

Probably.

Bec tries to get up, but stumbles. Rylan throws her arm over his shoulder.

BEC

My knight in shining armor.

RYLAN

Fuck off.

BEC

Be nice. I still haven't decided if we're getting together or not.

RYLAN

We can discuss it in the morning. Let's just get you home before Lexi realizes we're missing.

BEC

She probably already has.

RYLAN

My anxiety was already high enough without that thought in my head.

BEC

Well, here, let me fix that.

Bec kisses Rylan. Rylan pulls away, surprised.

RYLAN

So that's what that's like.

BEC

First kiss?

RYLAN

Yeah.

BEC

Not bad.

RYLAN

Shut up. Let's get you home.

Rylan helps her off stage.

SCENE 8: TREATMENT CENTER COMMON AREA

Bobby is sitting at the table. Rylan walks in.

RYLAN

Good morning, Bobby.

Bobby eyes go wide.

BOBBY

Hol' up. You can talk?

RYLAN

Yes.

BOBBY

What the fuck?

Bobby gets up from the table and shouts down the hall.

BOBBY

Hey! Rylan's talking!

KELLY

(offstage)

What?

Kelly comes running out.

KELLY

Rylan?

RYLAN

Hi, Kelly.

Kelly squeals with delight.

KELLY

Oh my goodness, hi!

Kelly runs up and hugs him. He is obviously not expecting this, but goes with it.

RYLAN

You know, I've been here the whole time.

KELLY

I know. But talking means you're making progress and I'm so happy for you.

RYLAN

Uh...thanks, I suppose?

BOBBY

Chill, Kel. Don't want to be level one tomorrow if Lexi or Jason walk in.

She lets go.

RYLAN

I like the enthusiasm though.

BOBBY

Okay, so what gives? Why now?

RYLAN

I'm not particularly looking to have this conversation. All I will say is that I've grown comfortable with speaking once again.

KELLY

Progress!

RYLAN

If that's what you want to call it, sure.

BOBBY

Well, I'm glad you've decided to join the rest of us.

RYLAN

I reiterate, I've been here the whole time. Just because I haven't directly spoken to any of you, doesn't mean that I wasn't around.

BOBBY

Yeah, but it's fuckin' weird, man. Like, I have never met anyone who just didn't talk.

RYLAN

What you consider weird, I consider normal.

BOBBY

You and I have different definitions of normal, bruv.

RYLAN

I'll accept that.

KELLY

I wonder what all the staff members are going to say about this.

Bec enters. Rylan looks up at her and smiles.

KELLY

Bec! Rylan's talking!

BEC

(faux surprise)

No way.

RYLAN

Hi, Bec.

BEC

Hi, Rylan. Your voice is deeper than I expected.

RYLAN

What? You didn't know if my balls had dropped or something?

BEC

(smiling)

No, I didn't, but thank you for settling that argument.

Rylan smiles. Lexi enters.

LEXI

Good morning, everyone.

RYLAN

Good morning.

Lexi looks like she just shit herself.

LEXI

Rylan. Your voice.

RYLAN

Jesus, yes it works. Let's move on.

LEXI

Watch it. You don't want to be level one for language like Bobby.

BOBBY

Alright, man, that shit ain't cool. Like, I get that I cuss a lot, but that level shit stays between you and me.

LEXI

I have permission to share whatever I wish.

BOBBY

Oh, fuck no you don't. Haven't you heard of a little thing called HIPAA? I'm protected from you telling my fellow inmates about how my treatment experience is going.

LEXI

That's enough Bobby. Please stop cursing or you will be level one again tomorrow.

BOBBY

Are you kidding me? Nah, fuck you, fam.

Bobby storms out.

LEXI
That settles that then. Kelly, can I steal you away for meds?

KELLY
Sure thing.

Lexi and Kelly leave.

RYLAN
How's the hangover?

BEC
Manageable. I asked Lexi for some ibuprofen when I took my meds.

RYLAN
Ooo! Meds! What kind of drugs are you taking?

BEC
Only the finest ecstasy pills.

RYLAN
I love that insurance is paying for the good stuff.

BEC
Right? I even hooked Medicaid up with my plug's number so they know where to get that high quality shit.

Rylan pulls a pack of cards out of his pocket.

RYLAN
Rummy?

BEC
Only if you scream when you call it.

RYLAN
I'll do my best.

Bec sits. Rylan shuffles and deals.

BEC
So. Why did you decide to start talking?

RYLAN
Not this again.

BEC
Sweet as you are, I couldn't have been the only reason you chose to speak.

RYLAN
You weren't, but I'm not entirely sure what you remember.

BEC
I'll let that forever be a mystery to you.

RYLAN

So be it.

BEC

I don't mean to press.

RYLAN

(sigh)

I know. This isn't personal. I just struggle with being honest with ... everyone.

BEC

You can trust me.

She takes his hand. He warms a little.

RYLAN

I wasn't lying when I said I wanted to talk to you. However, I suppose the overarching reason would be, I have trying to wrap my head around the idea that in order for me to be able to confront my problems, I need to be able to talk about them. Which is a problem when I don't speak.

BEC

Was it what Bobby said?

RYLAN

I wouldn't give him that much credit, but his comments were the straw that broke the camel's back.

BEC

I could tell. I'd never seen you so pissed before.

RYLAN

I don't get mad very often, but somehow he gets me seeing red more regularly than what I'm comfortable with. Especially with his masturbation habits.

BEC

Fuck you for putting that image in my head.

RYLAN

Suffer as I have suffered.

BEC

Okay, new topic. What closed you off in the first place?

RYLAN

Why did I stop speaking?

BEC

Yeah, I've always wondered.

RYLAN

(contemplating)

Let's just say that I was tired of being emotionally available and of giving others the power to hurt me. Closing my mouth allowed me the opportunity to be free of the perpetual torment of others, even though now I feel like I am less of a person for it.

BEC

You seem a bit eloquent for someone who's stuck in treatment.

RYLAN

I've been afforded time to think about how I see myself and how I see the world. Keeping quiet definitely helped with that.

BEC

Look at me.

RYLAN

(looking her in the eye)

Why?

BEC

Because I want your full attention as I say this. You are not any less of a person because you were doing what was best for you. You were taking care of you and that's what matters. You matter.

RYLAN

I disagree.

BEC

It's okay to be wrong sometimes.

RYLAN

Wrong is subjective.

BEC

I guess so.

RYLAN

Do you know what I'm talking about?

BEC

I'm trying to keep up.

RYLAN

Right and wrong mean different things to different people. You think you are right about me mattering while I disagree, and vice versa. It's subjective.

BEC

I feel like that long winded comment was only made to give you an excuse to shit on yourself.

RYLAN

Self-deprecation is a strong suit.

BEC

I don't know if I can be with someone who has such a low opinion of themselves.

RYLAN

How about someone who is working on it?

BEC
Only if he promises to be more open with me and is kind to himself when he's around me.

RYLAN
I feel like he would agree to such a compromise.

BEC
Then let's do it.

RYLAN
Okay.

They continue to play.

SCENE 9: TREATMENT CENTER COMMON AREA

Lexi, Bec, Kelly, and Chelsea are at various points in the room. Bec is dusting, Chelsea is tidying up around the room, and Kelly is sweeping.

LEXI
Keep it going, ladies. I want this room to be spotless.

CHELSEA
Must you treat us like we're prisoners?

LEXI
Well, you're not too far from it.

KELLY
We're not prisoners!

LEXI
Uh huh. Whatever you tell yourself.

BEC
This is pointless. Why do we even have to clean?

LEXI
Part of the program. If I see you haven't completed them to my expectations, you will lose points.

BEC
How does menial work translate to whether or not we get points?

LEXI
Because I said so. Now watch your tone. I don't like how aggressive you're getting.

Lexi exits.

BEC
Fuck this.

Bec throws the duster across the room.

KELLY
Bec! Why did you do that?

BEC
Because I'm tired of being treated like a problem child. Just because I'm here doesn't mean that they can treat me like I'm not a person.

CHELSEA
Unfortunately, darling, you give up your rights when you are admitted. Staff are allowed to ask you to do whatever it is they deem necessary. The bullshit part is the fact that they have the audacity to call it therapeutic.

KELLY
Chores aren't that bad.

BEC
It's more than just chores, Kel. I feel like the staff here don't give a damn.

KELLY
Jason cares. Lexi...

CHELSEA
... is an egotistical bitch who doesn't want anything to do with us.

KELLY
I wouldn't put it like that.

BEC
She's not too far off.

CHELSEA
The problem is that often times, staff members don't recognize that what they're doing is counterproductive to the resident's healing process.

BEC
Sounds like you're well informed.

CHELSEA
This isn't my first rodeo.

BEC
What do you mean?

CHELSEA
Story for a later time.

BEC
Now you sound like Rylan.

CHELSEA
The quiet boy. Interesting comparison.

BEC
He's more than just that.

KELLY
He opened up to you?

BEC
In a way. He's very secretive.

CHELSEA
Good. He shouldn't trust anyone here.

BEC
Fuck that. He can trust us.

CHELSEA
No, he can't. We're all just as fucked up as him.

BEC
We're not fucked up. Wc just have shit to deal with. There's a difference.

CHELSEA
Yes, there is.

KELLY
I agree with Bec. We're not broken, just wounded.

CHELSEA
If that's what you decided to believe.

BEC
Why are you here, Chelsea?

CHELSEA
I'm not going to share that. When I age out of here, I will put this all behind me.

BEC
You can't be serious, Chels. You're just going to wait it out? You probably have things you could be working on.

CHELSEA
Maybe. Who knows?

BEC
What's so wrong about dealing with your demons?

CHELSEA
Because there are none.

BEC
I beg to differ.

CHELSEA
If I remember correctly, I didn't fucking ask you.

BEC
Fine. So be it.

They continue to clean in silence.

KELLY
Okay, sweeping done. Time to go get Shannon.

BEC
Shannon?

KELLY
My mop!

BEC
Riiight.

Kelly exits with the broom.

BEC
I forgot she was in love with a mop.

CHELSEA
It's her pride and joy.

BEC
How does one even become attracted to an inanimate object?

CHELSEA
That's something you should ask her.

BEC
I don't know if that's appropriate.

CHELSEA
Asking flat out is better than letting the question bottle up. I'm sure she would be honest with you.

BEC
But that's her experience. It's not right to ask about that.

CHELSEA
You literally just asked me about mine.

BEC
Right but you seem more... in touch with yourself than Kelly does.

CHELSEA
So that means you can ask me and not her? Grow up.

BEC
That's not what I meant.

CHELSEA
Then say what you mean.

BEC

I don't want to trigger Kelly if it's not something she's comfortable talking about.

KELLY
(offstage)
What's triggering me?

Kelly reenters with a mop, evidently named Shannon.

BEC
Nothing. We were just discussing whether it was appropriate to ask you about Shannon.

KELLY
Oh. I mean...

BEC
We don't have to talk about it if you don't want to.

KELLY
It's okay. I actually haven't had an opportunity to tell any of my peers about Shan.

CHELSEA
Well now's a good a time as any to spill the beans.

KELLY
It may come as a struggle to understand, but I can sense Shannon has a soul. She has feelings and emotions. And I've been able to connect with her better than any person I've ever met.

BEC
How did you come across this?

KELLY
She was an accident. My parents bought her from Costco and brought her home one day. When she arrived, she had an aura that I sensed. It was unlike anything I had encountered. Instantly, I felt a connection with her that I had never felt with anyone.

BEC
What caused your attraction to her?

KELLY
Your guess is as good as mine. I mean, I didn't have almost any friends growing up. Building friendships was so hard for me. It didn't help that my parents were a problem for me and hurt me a lot throughout my childhood. With Shannon, it's just easy. I don't have to try so hard.

CHELSEA
It makes it easier when you can't communicate with her.

KELLY
While she may not speak, I am able to communicate with her. I sense her emotions and where she's at. Right now, she's frustrated about that comment.

CHELSEA
It wasn't ill willed. I just haven't encountered what you are experiencing.

BEC
We aren't trying to talk negatively about Shannon. We just want to understand.

KELLY
It's okay not to understand. I mean, in the long run it doesn't affect either of you. This is probably all in my head.

CHELSEA
But that doesn't mean it isn't real. Love is love. Whomever it is.

KELLY
How would you know?

CHELSEA
Because I'm not straight. I let myself feel love for whoever chooses to love me and I choose to love them back. Regardless of gender. In your case it's regardless of whether or not they're a person.

BEC
Bi?

CHELSEA
I'm pan. But I don't like labels. I just love.

KELLY
Did you ever receive push back from your parents?

CHELSEA
Yes. And fuck them for that.

KELLY
I just don't want to feel like it's wrong to feel this way about a mop, and so far I've been treated like a freak for it.

BEC
The good news is that you're not a freak.

CHELSEA
Yeah, that's Bobby.

KELLY
Oh, stop it.

BEC
You are allowed to love whom or whatever. Fuck what everyone else thinks. Are you happy with her?

KELLY
Incredibly.

BEC
That's what matters.

Kelly smiles. Lexi reenters.

LEXI
Kelly, did I tell you to mop?

KELLY
Well, no. But I thought it would be nice to -

LEXI
I don't care what you thought, you know you're not allowed to bring that out without permission. Go put it back. You've officially lost points.

Kelly looks defeated and exits.

SCENE 10: TREATMENT CENTER COMMON AREA

Rylan, Bec, Bobby, Kelly, and Chelsea are all playing a group game of Rummy. Lexi sits in the corner, watching them.

RYLAN
Let me end this.

Rylan plays cards from his hand until it is empty.

BOBBY
(throwing his cards down in frustration)
Damn, bro. How the hell you so good at this? That's like the fourth game you won.

RYLAN
Luck of the draw, I suppose.

BOBBY
That shit is wack.

LEXI
Bobby, watch the language.

BOBBY
Do you have to pick on me?

LEXI
I am paid to do so, yes.

RYLAN
I highly doubt antagonizing residents is part of the job description.

LEXI
Watch it, Rylan. Don't talk back to me.

KELLY
Lexi, that's not fair.

LEXI

You don't get to tell me what's fair. May I remind you that I am the staff and you are the resident. Now, all of you, drop it before I drop your points.

Rylan begins to shuffle cards. Jason enters.

JASON
Lex, do you want to cover Chelsea's meds?

LEXI
(to Chelsea)
Ready, kid?

CHELSEA
I don't have much of a choice. Now's a good a time as any.

They leave.

KELLY
Jason, why is Lexi allowed to be so mean to us?

JASON
She isn't.

BOBBY
Then why the fuck don't you do anything to stop it?

JASON
Because I don't have the power to, unfortunately. Not yet anyway.

BEC
Isn't there anything you can do about it? It's making all of this even harder.

JASON
I know. I don't approve of her methods either. Trust me that I'm making an effort to change things.

Rylan continues to shuffle cards.

KELLY
Jason, would you like to play with us?

JASON
What are you playing?

BOBBY
Oh hell nah. I ain't about to be playing with head narc himself.

JASON
You really see me as a narc?

BOBBY
No doy!

JASON
Interesting.

BEC
We're playing rummy.

JASON
That seems to be all you ever play. Ever consider changing it up?

BOBBY
All the real boy games are in the priv room, boss. Don't know if you know this but half of us aren't priv'd, and the other half is choosing to spend time with us.

JASON
I think we can make an exception, given there is staff supervision.

Jason walks out for a moment. Chelsea reenters.

CHELSEA
What'd I miss?

KELLY
Jason is treating everyone to a game from the priv room.

CHELSEA
Oh Jesus. If he picks Monopoly, I'm going AWOL.

BOBBY
If he picks Monopoly, I'm getting violent. That shit ruins lives.

KELLY
Jeez, those are such strong reactions.

BEC
I can see why. Monopoly is harsh.

RYLAN
Pretty sure my parents' last fight before they separated was because of Monopoly.

BOBBY
No shit?

RYLAN
If I remember correctly. This was at least 10 years ago.

BEC
You remember what they were fighting about?

RYLAN
No. All I remember is I had just collected all the money in free parking and then Dad got mad.

CHELSEA
See! Monopoly fucking sucks!

Jason reenters, carrying Apples to Apples and a speaker.

BOBBY

Oh thank fuck.

JASON
Bobby, come on, man. Do you have to swear so much?

BOBBY
I am the controller of my own self and if I wanna say fuck, I'm gonna say fuck. Sorry if you don't like it.

JASON
Most people aren't fans of such vulgarity.

BOBBY
Who are they to judge? They don't know me. They don't know why I do the things I do. I'm the only one who understands. I get to make the choices for myself.

JASON
I get where you're coming from, but society has set standards that we need to be able to abide by.

BOBBY
Fuck that noise. Just let me be myself. I'd rather people be pissed for seeing the true me than be shown the watered down version that you are trying to shove down my throat.

JASON
Fine. I won't try and convince you otherwise.

BOBBY
Best not.

BEC
So are we playing or what?

JASON
You guys shuffle and deal. I'm going to set up the speaker.

Jason plugs in and connects his Bluetooth.

KELLY
Ooh! Do we finally get a sneak peek of your Spotify playlists, Jason?

JASON
Yes, but only a select bit of it. Unfortunately, I have to keep it PG.

BOBBY
Bruh, if you start playing Coldplay, I'm hiding in my room for the rest of the day.

JASON
I got you, my friend.

Jason starts playing “Uptown Funk” by Bruno Mars.

BOBBY
Oh no, you didn't.

JASON
You a fan?

BOBBY
Of course, boss. I got my Bruno Mars impression down.

CHELSEA
Now this I have to see.

All of residents start enjoying the song and dance along. Bobby does a killer impression of Bruno Mars as he sings along. The song eventually ends.

JASON
Not bad, Bobby. I didn't know you had pipes on you.

BOBBY
Well, I'm full of surprises, aren't I?

JASON
Indeed you are.

Lexi enters.

LEXI
Rylan, your therapist is calling you back for your individual session. Bec, I need to steal you away for meds.

Rylan exits, Lexi and Bec begin to walk out.

LEXI
Oh, and Jason, upper management is expecting you to return their call.

JASON
Ah. I should go take care of that.

The three of them exit.

CHELSEA
Well that was certainly something.

KELLY
I agree. That was a lot of fun.

BOBBY
Shit wasn't fun. It was a show.

KELLY
What are you talking about? You absolutely killed that.

BOBBY
I know I did. But that was to throw him off my trail.

KELLY
What do you mean?

BOBBY

I'm running away.

CHELSEA

What?

BOBBY

Yeah! And I want you guys to come with me too.

KELLY

Bobby, that's a bad idea.

BOBBY

The fuck do you mean? It's great. I figured out how to disable the alarm system. We can just slip away.

KELLY

Maybe for a few hours. But you're talking about running away from everything. That's insane.

CHELSEA

I don't know, Kel. It makes a lot of sense.

KELLY

No, it doesn't. It'll ruin all of our discharges.

BOBBY

I don't even have a discharge date. They keep fucking with it. It's been pushed back so much that they've decided to completely remove it from my treatment plan.

KELLY

But that doesn't mean that you should run away!

CHELSEA

There's nothing here for us, except shitty rules and awful staff members.

KELLY

The staff members are here to help us!

BOBBY

Nah, fam. What have they ever done for me? Those inconsiderate fuckasses hang around and they watch the shit that I'm doing and they punish me. They don't care about me. They don't want to see me succeed. All they're here for is a fucking paycheck. Lexi is a psychotic bitch. She lives to watch me flounder. She goes out of her way to make my life fucking awful just so that she can rub herself off and feel good about herself. Does she even think about me? What I'm going through? Does she understand that she is making everything so much fucking worse for me? No. She doesn't. She is nothing but a lying, sadistic, pile of dog shit human being who I hope I never have to deal with again.

KELLY

But we still have Jason!

BOBBY

Kelly, you're missing the point. No matter what there are going to be staff members that are here only to fuck with you. If I wanted to be controlled and have my spirit crushed, I would've chosen the prison option of my sentence.

CHELSEA
Come with us. You'll have better odds out in the real world. Besides, you don't belong here.

KELLY
Of course I do. Objectophilia is a problem.

CHELSEA
Is it, though?

KELLY
Yes!

BOBBY
Sounds like bullshit to me.

KELLY
What are you talking about?

BOBBY
Who told you that being in love with a mop is a bad thing?

KELLY
It's just not socially accepted.

BOBBY
Yes, but who told you that?

KELLY
No one had to tell me that. It's something I knew.

BOBBY
Maybe that's how you were raised.

KELLY
What?

CHELSEA
Think about it. You came out to your parents right?

KELLY
Yeah.

CHELSEA
What was their response?

KELLY
It was... less than enthusiastic.

BOBBY
Don't give me that shit! They fucking hated it, didn't they? They sent you here!

KELLY
(hesitant)
Yeah...

CHELSEA
They're the ones that raised you to believe that there was something wrong with loving whoever.

KELLY
It's not just them though. When Bec got here, she was super grossed out when she found out.

BOBBY
Nah, she loved you. Where did you get that from?

CHELSEA
She knows that your sexuality does not define you as a person. But not everyone is like that. And unfortunately, your parents wanted to make you think that something was wrong with you, when in all reality, they didn't want you.

KELLY
(starting to realize, and starting to cry)
I... No. They're my parents, they love me.

BOBBY
If they loved you, they'd support you no matter what. That's why they left you here. They didn't want to be forced to live with someone they hated.

KELLY
Bobby. Stop. I don't want to talk about this anymore.

CHELSEA
Come with us. We can start over. We can create a life where you are surrounded by love and support.

BOBBY
What do you think?

Kelly considers this for a moment.

SCENE 11: TREATMENT CENTER COMMON AREA

Rylan and Bec sit on the couch together. She looks anxious. He does not look at her. He has a thousand yard stare.

BEC
It's not a bad idea.

RYLAN
I disagree.

BEC
Why? Wouldn't it be nice to finally get out of here?

RYLAN
Yes. But AWOL isn't exactly my first choice. Especially if we get caught, since it'll lead to us getting kicked out and sent to other treatment centers.

BEC
That's a bit over dramatic.

RYLAN
Really? You think that it's over dramatic? Tell me, what makes you believe that the outcome would be anything except getting royally fucked in the ass by the people in charge?

BEC
Oh come on. The consequences couldn't be that bad.

RYLAN
I am not willing to sacrifice my discharge just to play run away with people who are tired of this place.

BEC
I mean...

RYLAN
Do you want to talk about your feelings on the matter?

BEC
Not when you ask like that. You make it sound like nothing I say will change your mind.

RYLAN
Likely because it won't.

BEC
Did you end up getting stuck here because you don't listen to anyone except yourself?

Rylan finally looks at her.

RYLAN
No. I didn't, and don't you ever use that against me again.

BEC
I'm not using it against you. I'm saying an outside perspective might help you make a more thought-out decision.

RYLAN
A more thought-out decision? Because teenagers running around in the woods with no food, no shelter, no sort of support as they evade staff members from the treatment center they ran away from sounds like a wonderful idea.

BEC
You know what? Maybe it is a bad idea. But I want to do it.

RYLAN

If that's what you wish.

BEC

You won't come with me?

RYLAN

You know my thoughts on the matter. I'm not going to continue to talk about it.

BEC

Rylan, I really think that this could be good for us.

RYLAN

For us or for you?

BEC

Us! We wouldn't have to pretend out there. We could just be together.

RYLAN

What would we do? Where would we sleep?

BEC

We would figure it out.

RYLAN

Do you not hear how ludicrous this idea sounds?

BEC

It's not ludicrous. You're just being selfish.

RYLAN

Here's a grand idea. Maybe I want to be selfish. Maybe I want what's best for me. And maybe I don't want the one person who actually gives a shit about me to go. I'm not trying to put us at odds, I swear. All I'm worried about is what will happen in the long run. So what if they don't catch us? That doesn't mean that it would be any better. I'm having a hard time looking at myself in the mirror now and that's while being sheltered, fed, and given medication. Strip all of that away? I wouldn't last two days.

BEC

But we could make it together. I know we can do it.

RYLAN

I don't want to put us in a position where we would be jeopardize our discharges.

BEC

I still want you to think about it.

RYLAN

No.

BEC

Oh, come on.

RYLAN
I'm done having this conversation.

BEC
You don't get to just tap out. That's not how conversations work.

RYLAN
Don't push it, please.

BEC
No, you're being unreasonable.

RYLAN
If you so believe.

BEC
Do you try and confuse me with the words you choose?

RYLAN
Not especially.

BEC
Well, you suck at it.

RYLAN
So be it.

BEC
We're not done talking about this.

RYLAN
I am. If you're not, that's fine, but I will keep my mouth shut.

BEC
Don't you dare.

Rylan doesn't respond.

BEC
Rylan.

Rylan just looks at her.

BEC
You're being so fucking petty right now. Knock it off.

Rylan blinks.

BEC
God, I hate it when you're like this. This is so unreasonable.

Rylan continues to look forward.

BEC
Rylan, talk to me. We are settling this.

Rylan doesn't acknowledge her.

BEC

Listen here, you fucking mute. You don't get to just tap out when you don't feel like talking about things. You don't get to decide just to stop having a conversation when it no longer works for you. You have to grow a pair and talk about it like anyone else. Just because you have a tiny little scar on your back doesn't mean that you are any better than the rest of us. You are just as filthy and broken and fucked up as the rest of us. You just happen to wear the pain on your skin. So get off your fucking high horse and join everyone else.

Rylan doesn't respond.

BEC

ARGH!

Bec topples a bookshelf. Rylan gets up and looks at her.

RYLAN

Let's recap. You just started screaming and cursing at me as loud as you could, you trivialized my experience outside of the treatment center and ridiculed me because of it, and you toppled a bookshelf in anger all because of the fact that I wouldn't continue a conversation that I had no interest in pursuing and yet I'M the unreasonable one? Huh. Maybe I really didn't think our relationship through as much as I should've, did I?

Rylan leaves before Bec has a chance to say anything.

BLACK OUT

SCENE 12: RYLAN'S BEDROOM

Immediately following the previous scene, Rylan enters his bedroom. He starts punching the bed as hard as he can. After feeling less than satisfied he starts to break things in his room. Eventually he moves into screaming into a pillow. He removes the pillow and starts crying. Jason knocks on his door.

JASON

Rylan?

RYLAN

The. Fuck. Do. You. Want?

JASON

What's going on?

RYLAN

Does it matter?

JASON

It does to me. Can we talk?

RYLAN

I'd rather not.

JASON

Unfortunately, bud, I'm gonna have to come in and check as safety precautions.

RYLAN

(sighing)

Door's open.

Jason enters the room.

JASON

This looks about right.

RYLAN

Can I help you? I would rather have my emotional meltdown not have any witnesses.

JASON

Well, help me help you. What's going on?

RYLAN

I'd rather not get into it.

JASON

Okay. Let's just sit then.

They sit for a moment.

RYLAN

You really don't have to do this.

JASON

I know. I want to.

RYLAN

I highly doubt that.

JASON

What gives you that perspective?

RYLAN

You're not here to help me, you enjoy watching us squirm.

JASON

I actually find it appalling. I try to help you cope with what you're feeling so you can have the tools to deal with the emotions in the future.

RYLAN

I can see right through that goody two shoes act. Don't think you're getting a word out of me.

JASON

You don't trust me?

RYLAN
You haven't exactly attempted to prove you're worth trusting.

JASON
What do you think I'm doing right now?

RYLAN
Instigating me.

JASON
Quite the opposite. And I think you're smart enough to tell the difference.

RYLAN
Whatever you say.

Rylan sits solemnly for a moment.

JASON
Do you even want help?

RYLAN
I'm actually contemplating that right now.

JASON
Do you see any benefits against it?

RYLAN
Not especially, though it would make me feel better.

JASON
Right now? Or forever?

RYLAN
Nothing will make me feel better in the long run.

JASON
Accepting help would.

RYLAN
No. It wouldn't. It would make me nothing more than putty in the hands of whoever I open up to.

JASON
You're afraid of losing control.

RYLAN
Yes.

JASON
You just have to be selective with what you share with whom.

RYLAN
What do you think I've been doing?

JASON

I've noticed, this is the point where you have to take a leap of faith and know that the person sitting in front of you, who wants with every fiber of his being to help you, is not going to take advantage of you or hurt you.

RYLAN
You know how many people have said that to me? That they were never going to hurt or take advantage of me? I stopped counting a long time ago.

JASON
I'm not them.

RYLAN
You have yet to prove that.

JASON
Fine. I'll throw some skin in the game. I lied to you.

RYLAN
And yet you want me to trust you?

JASON
Remember that first night after you woke up screaming?

RYLAN
Well... yeah. A little hard to forget that that was the first impression I made.

JASON
(chuckle)
It was a pretty great entrance.

RYLAN
Get out.

JASON
I'm just kidding. There is a reason why I'm bringing it up.

RYLAN
If that's the case, then please bring us to the point.

JASON
I told you that night that I knew what it was like because I've seen kids come and go, but I wasn't being entirely truthful. I know what it's like because I've been in treatment.

RYLAN
Excuse me?

JASON
Years ago. I was dealing with the same thing. People screwed me over and hurt me. I was tired of trying to pretend that I was okay as everyone sucked the life out of me. So I was sent to a place like this. When I got in, I messed around, I didn't care about receiving help. I just thought treatment would be a short-term thing. Then I realized in order for things to change, I had to be transparent and open. I had to

want the help. So I'm going to ask you right now. If you say no, I will walk out that door and I will be nothing more than a staff member to you. Do you want help?

RYLAN

I... I don't think I have any other option.

JASON

You could say no.

RYLAN

What good will that do for me?

JASON

Glad you're catching on.

RYLAN

I don't want to have my efforts be in vain. I just want to be okay.

JASON

Well, first you have to learn that it's okay to not be okay.

RYLAN

Sounds contradictory.

JASON

And yet there is still wisdom in it. Life is going to push you around, you just gotta learn to take the punches. You're going to be hurt, the trick is not minding that it hurts.

RYLAN

I guess.

JASON

You're not going to be okay through this conversation. But you need to remain present and allow yourself to be transparent. We need to break through.

RYLAN

I will try my best.

JASON

So what's going on?

RYLAN

Well... it's a long story. Bec and I have been getting friendly.

JASON

We've noticed.

RYLAN

I figured.

JASON

Would you like my thoughts on the matter?

RYLAN

Would you be disappointed if I said I didn't give a shit?

JASON
No, but I might take some points away for language.

RYLAN
Fair enough. So, we've been getting friendly and we had a huge argument. She was telling me something I didn't want to hear and I didn't have the energy to fight back, so I went quiet. She completely blew up and started using my issues against me. It shook me to the core.

JASON
I'm sorry that happened.

RYLAN
I'm tired of being the problem. I'm tired of people thinking that everything bad that's happening is my fault, especially when it's people I care about.

JASON
Not everything is your fault.

RYLAN
My mother would tell you differently.

JASON
Tell me about her.

RYLAN
It doesn't matter.

JASON
You wouldn't have brought her up if it didn't matter.

RYLAN
I really don't like talking about her.

JASON
Why not?

RYLAN
Because... I'm afraid of her.

JASON
Okay.

RYLAN
She thought that I was the worst thing that happened to her. Said she should have had me aborted. I was the cause of all her problems.

JASON
No, you weren't. You were a gift.

RYLAN
I wasn't a gift. And she reminded me of that with gifts of her own.

JASON

What does that mean?

RYLAN

My mother had... other uses for a belt than just holding her pants up.

JASON

Ah. I see.

RYLAN

I've prayed for a better mom, hell, just a different one. I wanted something else, someone else to come and love me. I tried everything in my power to be the best son I could, but all I ever got was blame. She was convinced she had a shitty life because she was stuck with me. I've come to recognize that simply because things could've been different, doesn't mean that they would've been better.

JASON

Is she still in your life?

RYLAN

No. But her actions still affect me to this day. Every relationship I have had with another human being has echoed that one. I allow others to step on me and steal everything I have, and I let them because if I say no, they'll leave just like she did.

JASON

You just haven't found the right people.

RYLAN

Nobody cares about me. If they do, they're just pretending.

JASON

I'm not pretending. Nor do I think Bec is.

RYLAN

She is.

JASON

No, I think she spoke from strong emotion. On the occasions I've talked to her, she has proven to be a kindhearted individual, yet she speaks harshly when she's fired up.

RYLAN

The intensity is what scares me. That's when she allows herself to say things that are mean and cruel.

JASON

I genuinely don't think she meant it. She is quick to apologize for things like that.

RYLAN

But what if this happens again?

JASON

I think you're going to need to trust your instincts on this one. If that means she shouldn't be in your life, that's up to you. From my perspective, she's been one of your only motivations. You're picky. If she is someone you can talk to, then roll with it. At least for the sake of having someone you trust to talk to. That being said, that doesn't mean she has a right to talk down to you. That's a conversation you need to have with her.

RYLAN
I'm scared of falling from the leap of faith trusting her would be.

JASON
Here's a secret: we all are. That's the risk. High risk, high reward.

Jason moves to the door.

JASON
If you need to talk anymore, I'm here for you.

RYLAN
Thank you.

SCENE 13: TREATMENT CENTER COMMON AREA

Immediately following her side of the previous scene. Bec sits on the couch, crying softly. Chelsea enters.

CHELSEA
Oh, well, we can't have this, now can we?

She walks over to Bec, who looks up at her, and sits on the couch.

BEC
I'd rather not, if you don't mind.

CHELSEA
Oh, cut the crap. You do better when you vent your feelings.

BEC
No, I don't.

CHELSEA
Please, every week you get all worked up over the dumbest things, then when you have individual therapy, you always snap out of it. It's okay, most of us are the same.

BEC
Look, I don't want to talk about it, Chels. Okay? I'm tired and I just want to be alone.

CHELSEA
(tutting)
You won't feel better with an attitude like that.

BEC
Fuck off. Please.

CHELSEA

Why are you crying?

BEC

It doesn't matter.

CHELSEA

Allow me to decide whether that is the case.

BEC

You don't get to hear these things.

CHELSEA

Why not?

BEC

"I don't want juvenile delinquents to know my personal information."

CHELSEA

Hey, you can't steal that from me. It's copyrighted material.

BEC

You have no right to ask me, especially with how secretive you been about your mental space, so please, save us both some time and leave me be.

Chelsea doesn't say anything at first. She chews her words, deciding what the best way to say what she means is.

CHELSEA

I have been in treatment for approximately 3 years, 2 months, 3 weeks, and 2 days. This is my third treatment center.

BEC

What?

CHELSEA

I was originally admitted because I had a problem with my parents. We fought constantly. I was frustrated with the way they were treating me. It never felt like I was good enough for either of them. They had Ivy League expectations, while I could only provide community college results.

BEC

I thought you said you had a great relationship with your parents?

CHELSEA

Would you believe me if I told you I was lying?

BEC

I wouldn't put it past you.

CHELSEA

I used to run away. Like a lot. Sometimes it would be to my girlfriend's house, other times to my cousin's. She's older and she understood when I needed to come stay.

BEC
Sounds like a real homie.

CHELSEA
So I thought. Eventually, everyone became tired of my bullshit, so I was sent here, kicking and screaming. There isn't anything wrong with me.

BEC
I'd beg to differ.

CHELSEA
As much as I would love to see that, you would be groveling for nothing.

BEC
What was the last straw?

CHELSEA
I'm not getting into it. All I'll say is that I have never heard so much bullshit regarding goddamn spaghetti sauce.

BEC
And has anything gotten better?

CHELSEA
Fuck no. This place is a hellhole. I am not going to sell out who I am because someone else thinks there's something wrong with me.

BEC
You should listen to the professionals. They're here to help you.

CHELSEA
(sarcastically)
Yeah, okay.

BEC
I'm serious.

CHELSEA
Me too. No person who has been in my life during this treatment experience has actually cared about me. I haven't been able to trust anyone. Honestly, at this point, I'm going to be here until I turn 18, and that is something I am perfectly okay with, because I know that I am my best self and if people want to think that's wrong, they can fuck right off.

BEC
I don't think that's true.

CHELSEA
True as the sky is blue.

BEC
You don't believe that.

CHELSEA

Sure I do.

BEC
You may have the others fooled, but I can tell when you're lying.

CHELSEA
Whatever you believe to be true.

BEC
You should open yourself up more.

CHELSEA
I just did. And now, in return, I expect you to do the same.

BEC
(sighing)
Rylan and I...

CHELSEA
Have been swapping spit for a bit? Yeah, we know.

BEC
How did you -

CHELSEA
Rylan slipped it to Bobby and Bobert can't keep his mouth shut.

BEC
Fuckin' Bobby.

CHELSEA
Fuckin' Bobby. Anyway...

BEC
We've been hanging out for a bit, and I really like him. He's kind to me and I really enjoy talking to him.

CHELSEA
Now that he can talk.

BEC
Yes. He's incredibly intelligent, he uses these big words that I don't always understand and it's so cute and -

CHELSEA
BARF. Move on already, I want that hot tea.

BEC
So we were talking about the plan and he didn't think it was a good idea. He became incredibly frustrated with me and wouldn't listen to what I had to say. He just shut me out of the conversation and stopped talking to me.

CHELSEA
Dick.

BEC

He's not. He was right. I was wrong to get mad at him. It's just so frustrating. He's great but if we don't learn how to communicate -

Rylan starts to walk in, but sees them and listens in.

BEC

- I don't think my relationship with him is going to last.

RYLAN

Not going to last huh?

Rylan reveals himself. Bec and Chelsea look shocked.

BEC

Rylan.

RYLAN

I came out here to apologize and you elect to share that you want to break up? Really? Fuck this.

Rylan leaves.

SCENE 14: RYLAN'S BEDROOM

Rylan is furiously packing his clothes. Bec comes in.

BEC

Rylan, I'm sorry. That's not what I meant.

Rylan is unfazed.

BEC

Come on, talk to me.

Rylan doesn't acknowledge her. Chelsea comes up to the door and listens in.

BEC

If you had heard the rest of the conversation, you would know that I was just explaining that I want to learn to communicate with you. This is a misunderstanding.

Rylan continues to ignore her.

BEC

Rylan, please talk to me. I'm sorry. Don't do this.

Rylan continues to pack. Bobby sees Chelsea, but she makes a motion to indicate "I'm listening in." He looks disgruntled but listens with her

BEC

Rylan.

Rylan stands up and walks over to her.

RYLAN
I have nothing to say to you.

Rylan gets back to packing. Bobby and Chelsea look astonished.

BEC
Come on, that's not fair.

Rylan doesn't acknowledge her. Bobby leaves Chelsea outside and enters the room.

BOBBY
What's goin' on?

RYLAN
(to Bobby)
When do we leave?

BOBBY
You forreal?

RYLAN
Absolutely.

BOBBY
20 minutes?

RYLAN
Excellent.

BEC
Rylan, don't go.

RYLAN
(without looking at her)
Bec, just leave now. You're making a fool of yourself by continuing your one-sided conversation.

Rylan and Bobby pack. Bec is left speechless. She exits.

SCENE 15: TREATMENT CENTER COMMON AREA

Bobby and Rylan enter with packed bags.

BOBBY
The front door alarm shouldn't be turned on. Let's slip out before they see us.

RYLAN
I thought we were leaving out the window?

BOBBY
Nah, this is easier.

RYLAN
What if they catch us?

BOBBY
There's no one around. We're fine.

LEXI
(off stage)
You sure about that?

Jason, Lexi, Bec, and Kelly come in.

BOBBY
Fuck me.

BEC
No thanks.

Rylan scowls at her.

LEXI
Did you really think we were going to let you leave?

BOBBY
Which one of y'all snitched?

JASON
Nobody snitched. Kelly and Bec were concerned for your wellbeing and brought the plan to our attention.

RYLAN
(to Bobby)
You're right. They don't care about us.

KELLY
Yes, we do.

BOBBY
Oh really? Since when?

LEXI
That doesn't matter. You aren't going anywhere.

BOBBY
Yeah, and who's finna stop me?

JASON
I would like to attempt to. But leaving is your choice.

LEXI
(as though he just committed sacrilege)
No, it isn't.

JASON
Technically speaking, it is. We can't stop them from going. We can call the police if they leave and are gone longer than 20 minutes, but there is nothing that we are allowed to do to stop them from going AWOL.

KELLY

That seems impractical.

Jason shrugs.

BOBBY

Nah, man. I'm leaving.

JASON

What makes you want to go?

BOBBY

This. All of this. The food. The therapy. Lexi. I can't take it anymore.

LEXI

Oh, you little -

Jason stops her there with one look. She shuts up immediately.

JASON

Let's just take a minute and think about this.

BOBBY

I've done enough thinking. I'm miserable here. I thought coming here would make my life better but instead I'm stuck with people who can't stand me, staff members who keep fucking with me, and an environment that forces me to sit with myself.

JASON

Do you not like sitting with yourself?

BOBBY

No. I really don't.

JASON

Why not?

BOBBY

Because I hate myself, don't you understand?

JASON

Help me understand.

BOBBY

No.

JASON

Bobby, I just want to help.

BOBBY

Then don't! That's how you help.

JASON

Seems like you don't want to face the problem.

RYLAN

Does anybody?

JASON

Why are you leaving, Rylan?

RYLAN

Similar reasons to Bobby.

JASON

Surely, a staff member hasn't belittled you.

RYLAN

I can't confirm or deny the existence of such belittlement considering the current people in this room.

Everyone looks at Lexi.

LEXI

What?

JASON

This seems so unlike you.

RYLAN

Then you don't know me at all.

JASON

I think we both know you don't believe that.

RYLAN

Oh, yeah? And why do you think that? Simply because I had one insignificant conversation with you, you now believe you know everything about me.

JASON

I never said I did.

RYLAN

Yes, but it's what you were thinking.

JASON

Wrong.

RYLAN

Oh, yeah? Then what was it you were pondering?

JASON

I was thinking that I see an incredible young man throwing away his future because he is scared of opening up, and because he feels betrayed by those he trusted.

RYLAN

That only further confirms my point.

JASON

Then go. But know that you are only making things worse for yourself.

Chelsea runs into the room.

CHELSEA
Did I miss it? Did they bolt?

BEC
Late to the party. As usual.

CHELSEA
What did you expect?

RYLAN
I'm tired of this. Bobby, let's go.

BEC
Rylan, wait.

RYLAN
I'm not talking to you.

BEC
Think about what you're doing.

RYLAN
What I'm doing is getting the hell away from you as fast as I can.

BEC
You're making a rash decision. This isn't like you.

RYLAN
How would you know? You didn't even allow yourself the opportunity to get to know me before you realized you ought to ditch me.

BEC
I wasn't going to ditch you. I was hurt about our fight and you heard a select part of the conversation out of context.

RYLAN
No, I didn't. You said you didn't think your relationship with me wasn't going to last.

BEC
I was venting. I was speaking my own personal truth into the universe because I knew that would help me feel better. I was trying to figure out what I was feeling so I could talk to you like a levelheaded person. You didn't deserve my anger and I fucked up. I was scared of losing you and it frustrated me, but that doesn't mean I should've taken it out on you. I'm sorry.

Rylan is taken aback.

RYLAN
No. You don't get to apologize. You absolutely negated my entire emotional experience. You were going to leave me.

BEC
I wasn't going to leave you.

RYLAN

Yes you were. And now I have to go. I can't give you the opportunity to leave me. I have to leave you.

BEC

Rylan, please. Stay here. I want you here. I need you. Please don't leave me.

Her words hit Rylan hard, and he starts crying.

BEC

Please stay.

RYLAN
(quietly, still crying)

Okay.

Rylan sits. Bec tries to comfort him.

RYLAN

Don't. Touch. Me.

Rylan stares daggers at her. Bec backs off.

BOBBY

What the fuck, Rylan?

JASON

Come on, Bobby. Do you really blame him?

BOBBY
(sighing in frustration)

Nah, I guess not.

JASON

Are you still going?

BOBBY

No. But we need to have ourselves a conversation about Lexi.

JASON

I agree.

LEXI

What?

JASON

The way you have continually belittled our residents is unprofessional and uncalled for.

LEXI

What are you talking about? I am only doing what I was trained to do.

JASON

And you have. However, you have also specifically targeted Bobby on multiple occasions. As such, your last day on unit will be today.

LEXI
You're firing me?

JASON
Yes.

LEXI
You don't have the authority.

JASON
Actually, yes I do. As manager of the unit, I report everything to upper management. I spoke with them about how your behavior has been inappropriate, and frankly, they agree with me. I received permission to terminate your position today. I can show the email they sent me to you if you'd like.

LEXI
(fuming)
Fuck this. Fuck you, Jason.
(she turns and faces all the residents individually)
Fuck you. Fuck you. Fuck you. Fuck you.
(referring to Bobby)
And especially fuck you, Robert.

BOBBY
You sound pretty confident for a bitch who just lost her job.

Lexi lunges at Bobby. Before she can reach him, Jason steps between them.

JASON
Don't you fucking dare.

Jason stands his ground. Lexi backs off.

JASON
Seeing as you have tried to attack one of my residents, I will now ask you to leave. If you don't, I will put you in a hold and call security.

LEXI
(to Jason)
Fucking asswipe.

She leaves, spitting on Jason as she walks out.

BOBBY
You aight?

JASON
I'm fine. I'm glad that garbage human being is out of the unit.

BOBBY
It's not like her leaving is finna change anything.

JASON
I mean, I would hope it would provide you a little more comfort here.

BOBBY
Why does my comfort matter? Y'all don't even like me anyway.

BEC
What are you talking about?

JASON
Dude, you serious? I love working with you.

BOBBY
Huh?

JASON
Truly. You're hysterical. I enjoy our conversations together.

BOBBY
Nah, man. You playin'.

BEC
I don't think he is. And honestly, I agree with him.

BOBBY
Get outta here.

KELLY
Same here. You've made my stay here so much more enjoyable.

BOBBY
Really?

RYLAN
Yep. You've been the best roommate when you're not masturbating while I'm still awake.

BOBBY
So don't listen.

RYLAN
You sleep 10 feet away from me. And it's not exactly easy to sleep when you hear "Oh fuck yeah, Kate," coming from your side of the room.

Bobby recoils a bit. Chelsea shifts a bit.

BOBBY
(to Chelsea)
Got anything to say?

Chelsea looks up at him.

CHELSEA
You're a loudmouth, vulgar, and quite often an incredibly inappropriate human being... but the good thing about that is some of the best people are.

BOBBY
I think that's the closest thing to a compliment I'll ever hear come outta your mouth.

CHELSEA

Don't get used to it.

BOBBY

(smiling)

I'll try not to.

Bobby drops his bags and sits on the couch.

BOBBY

Y'know, I've always been a one-man wolf pack kinda guy. I never thought anyone actually liked me, not even my family. Guess I realized that the only family I need is y'all.

BEC

We love you, Bobby.

Scattered agreement.

BOBBY

I love y'all too.

SCENE 16: TREATMENT CENTER COMMON AREA

The board reads "August 4th". Bec, Rylan, Chelsea, and Bobby all sit on the couches. Jason sits at the staff table. Kelly stands, in front of him, holding a paper.

JASON

Level 4. Congratulations on your discharge.

KELLY

Thank you, Jason.

JASON

Alright, everyone, that's it for levels. Free time. We don't have group today.

Everyone expresses relief. Jason packs up the binder.

CHELSEA

Well, Kelly, it's been real, but sleep is calling my name.

Chelsea hugs Kelly.

CHELSEA

Good luck out there. And remember, love is love. Fuck anyone who disagrees.

KELLY

Thanks, Chels.

Chelsea leaves. Jason gets up.

JASON

Bobby, before you hop too far into free time, you still have an extra chore.

BOBBY
(rolling his eyes)
Fine. Imma go scrubs some toilets, then.

Bobby and Jason both leave.

BEC
(to Kelly)
You excited?

KELLY
Yeah! Little nervous, but I'm ready to get back out into the world.

RYLAN
Are you going back to your parents?

KELLY
Well... no. They've actually requested that I be taken somewhere else.

BEC
Oh no.

KELLY
Yeah.

RYLAN
Fuck them.

KELLY
Rylan.

RYLAN
I'm serious. If they can't get over a small detail about you, instead creating a toxic environment where they make you feel inadequate then you're better off without them.

KELLY
Yeah, but they're my parents.

RYLAN
Parents can be awful too. They've made their stance clear. And you know what? You're better than them. You are kind and loving. You are one of the best people I know. It's their loss.

KELLY
Thank you.

JASON
(off stage)
Kelly, the Jennings are here.

KELLY
That's my cue.

They all stand up. They each take turns hugging, and Kelly leaves. Rylan and Bec look at each other. It is the first time they've spoken since he almost ran.

RYLAN

Hey.

BEC

Hey.

Rylan smiles at her.

BEC

I thought you never wanted to speak to me again.

RYLAN

Things change.

BEC

I suppose so.

RYLAN

I don't hate you, Bec.

BEC

I know. I just... didn't realize that until just now.

RYLAN

I told you I didn't want to talk then. I didn't mean to make you feel like I wasn't going to speak to you forever.

BEC

I wish you had clarified.

RYLAN

I apologize. I'm not very good at words sometimes.

BEC

Shut the hell up, you legitimately have the largest vocabulary out of anyone I've ever known.

RYLAN

You need to meet more people then.

BEC

Take the compliment.

RYLAN

If I must.

BEC

Why are you so hard on yourself?

RYLAN

Because it's easy.

BEC

Because you don't want to change your bad habits.

RYLAN

That's an overgeneralization.

BEC

Then tell me the real answer.

RYLAN

(sighing)

Because it's all I've ever known.

BEC

What do you mean?

RYLAN

I insult myself because of the feedback loop that I was put through as a kid. My mother would tell me all of these awful things about myself and I would repeat them at school because it would get a laugh out of my peers. No one ever corrected me and no one has ever made me believe that I was genuinely worth anything so it became hard for me to accept compliments, because I always thought the other person was fucking with me.

BEC

Listen to me. You are worthy of love. You are smart and kind and funny as hell when you don't put the front up.

RYLAN

Yeah, but I put a front up for a reason. I refuse to let anyone get close to me.

BEC

I know.

A beat.

RYLAN

I don't do it because I want to hurt you.

BEC

You don't need to explain anything. I get it.

RYLAN

No, I do. Bec, I want to trust you. I want to tell you everything that goes on in my mind. I want to be your best friend and confide in you. I just haven't yet because all of this is so fucking scary to me. I am terrified because in all of my life I haven't let anyone in and you are the first person who I actually want to tell things to.

BEC

Why me?

RYLAN

I don't know why. What I do know is that I am taking a leap. I'm going face first into the abyss. Throughout my life, I have wondered when the right time to jump would be, and frankly I never thought that it would come. The idea of jumping into something where I don't know what is going to happen scares me, but I'm tired of being alone. I'm gonna jump. I'm not going to know where I'm landing or how long I'll be falling for. What I do know is you'll be by my side, and that alone lets me know that everything will be fine.

BEC

I'm not going anywhere. If you fall, we'll fall together.

RYLAN

Okay.

BEC

I need you, Rylan Hayes.

RYLAN

You don't need me.

BEC

I want to need you.

RYLAN

That's unhealthy.

BEC

Then help me reframe it. You're the one who knows how to make insane thoughts and emotions into cohesive sentences.

RYLAN

I hope you will never need me. Instead, I hope you want me.

BEC

See, I told you you're good with words.

RYLAN

Sometimes. I think it's more I just overthink things and thus have the opportunity to present information in whatever way I see best.

BEC

You're a fucking nerd.

RYLAN

That's not an incorrect assertion. But you're the one who's dating the nerd.

BEC

We're still together?

RYLAN

I mean... if you want to. What do you think?

BEC
(off put by the question)
Huh... Um... I think...
(wickedly grinning)
I think we should play rummy.

RYLAN
What?

BEC
Rummy.

RYLAN
Right, I heard you. But what about -

BEC
Rummy.

RYLAN
Yes, I understand. But -

BEC
Let's just play. We can figure it all out later.

RYLAN
But -

Bec kisses him.

BEC
Rummy.

RYLAN
(confused)
I suppose I could go a round or two.

Bec grabs a deck from her pocket.

BEC
Good, cause I've missed kicking your ass.

RYLAN
Oh, please. We all know I will always come out on top. I'm the rummy champion on unit.

BEC
Don't be so cocky. There are still many games left to play, babe.

Bec shuffles the cards and deals out 7 cards to herself and Rylan. They begin to play.

END OF PLAY

www.ingramcontent.com/pod-product-compliance
Lightning Source LLC
LaVergne TN
LVHW080817170826
845678LV00011B/2041

9798848846966